For Sarah Wheeler —MB

For Patrick —GP

VIKING

An imprint of Penguin Random House LLC, New York

First published in the United States of America by Viking,
an imprint of Penguin Random House LLC, 2020

Text copyright © 2020 by Mac Barnett
Illustrations copyright © 2020 by Greg Pizzoli

Viking & colophon is a registered trademark of Penguin Random House LLC.
Visit us online at penguinrandomhouse.com

LIBRARY OF CONGRESS CATALOGING-IN-PUBLICATION DATA IS AVAILABLE
ISBN 9780593113943

Manufactured in China

Book design by Greg Pizzoli and Jim Hoover   Set in Clarion MT Pro

10   9   8   7   6   5   4   3   2   1

TOO MANY JACKS

Mac Barnett & Greg Pizzoli

Viking

1.

A NICE GIFT

Look! The Lady got
Jack a nice gift!

What's in that box?
What is that gift?

It's a lab kit!

A lab kit for Jack!

Jack, don't be sad.

What did you wish for?

Jack, it can't
always be snacks.

You can't have lipstick.
You make a mess.

Just go play
with your kit!

Not in the house, Jack.

Out there, in the shed.

Wait, give me that test tube.

And that fuse.

OK, Jack.

2.

THE SHED

Jack works in the shed.

The shed is his lab.

Jack has been
in there all day.

He must love
that gift!

What was that bang?

What was that crash?

3.

IT HAS BEEN FIVE DAYS

Jack is still in his lab.

Jack, come out here!
We will give you a snack.

Jack, you look proud.

Jack, you look glad.

Show us what you
made in your lab.

Oh my!

Jack made a . . . Jack.

Hi, Jack!
And hi, Jack!

Oh, hi, Jack and Jack
and Jack and . . . wow.

I think this is bad.

4.

THE PILE
OF STUFF

Hide all your lipstick!
Hide all your snacks!
Lock up your house!
Lock up the bank!

Oh, it's no use.

The Jacks have gone wild.

They bring Jack a pile
of stuff that he wants.

Rex, do not wag.

Do not wag your tail
at all these Jacks.

Can't you see that this is bad?

It is too many Jacks.

One Jack is fine.

Two Jacks is a lot.

But this many Jacks
is too many Jacks.

That pile is huge!
Jack, give that stuff back.

That is all the
town's snacks.
All the lipstick.

The cash.

But these Jacks are not done.

What will they do next?

5.

IT HAS BEEN FIVE WEEKS

Now those Jacks
rule the town.

The Jacks are
in charge.

The town is a mess.

This is too much.

Too much even for Jack.

He hides with the Lady
and Rex in the shed.

They read books.

They play cards.

They miss the sun.

Oh no!
A knock at the door.

It is the Jacks!

The Jacks are out there,
and they want to break in.

There is a crack!

There is a smash!

We need a plan now!

We need a plan.

6.

THE PLAN

Look! Jack made a plan.

If those Jacks get wet,
their wires will fry!

But we need something wet.

We need something big.

What is wet? What is big?

It might even be red.

Rex! Your tongue is big!
Your tongue is wet!
Your tongue is red!

Rex, go lick those Jacks.

Rex licks all the Jacks!
Their wires go ZAP!

Jack after Jack gets
fried by his licks.

Rex, you saved the day!

OK, you saved
it too, Jack.

The Jacks are all fried.
Now there is only one Jack.

That feels just right.

We are good with one Jack.

7.

A THANK-YOU GIFT

The town puts a statue of
Rex in the town square.

There are free snacks,
and there is lipstick for Jack.

It is a big day!
We should count to three,
then take off the sheet!
1, 2, 3!

Oh. It is a big, red tongue.

OUR HERO

That is weird and gross.

But it is also kind of nice.

A big, red tongue
in the town square.

Rex! Do not lick that!

Do not lick your own tongue!

Oh, fine. Let him lick.

Thank you, Rex.
Thank you, Jack.

HOW TO DRAW...
ROBOT JACK!

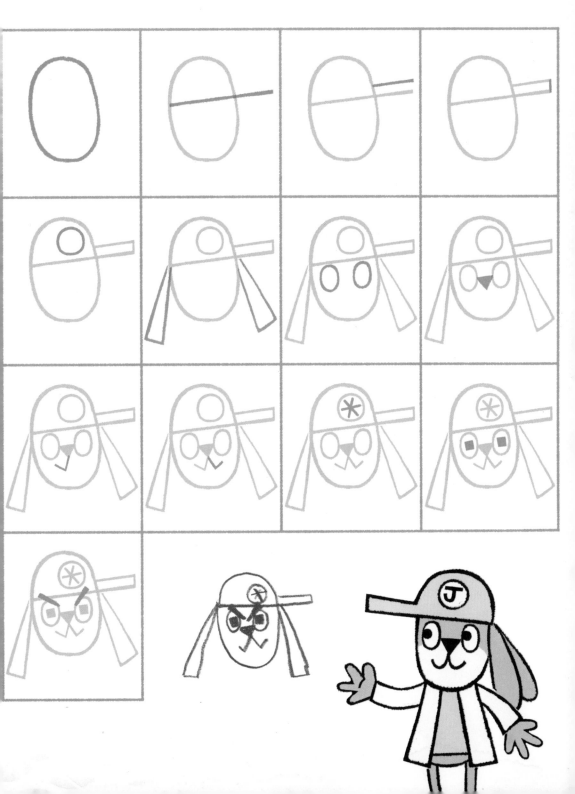